written by
Marcela Ferreira

illustrated by
Brian Lambert

the Treasure

MAGIC CAT PUBLISHING

Once, atop a cold, dark mountain, beneath eight tall, scraggly trees, there was an old wooden chest. And in that chest, there was a **treasure** so special that it could make your **dreams** come true.

Or so it was said.

Hare, longing for a
life beyond **grazing**,

hiding

and **boxing**,

set off to find it.

But the mountain was **steep**,
and **creepy**, and **cold**.
And the higher she went,
the harder it was
to climb.

Hare looked for shelter, when,
'Psssssttttt,' said a voice from a cave.
And in the cave, there was a Bear.
'Come and get dry,' he growled.

Hare stared at his **claws**

and his **teeth,**

and the glint
in his **eyes,**

and hesitated
before stepping inside,

where Bear offered her tea.

'I'm looking for the **treasure**,'
said Bear, 'but I got lost, and
no one would help me.'

Hare turned to the claws, and
the teeth and the eyes... and the tea.
'Maybe... we can look together?'
she said.

Bear grinned, and they shook paws.

Outside, the wind howled,
and the rain fell, and yet the
animals slept soundly.

The next day, Bear and Hare set off early.
And the mountain was **steep**,
and **creepy**, and **cold**.

But the animals thought only of the **treasure**, and how it could make their dreams come true.

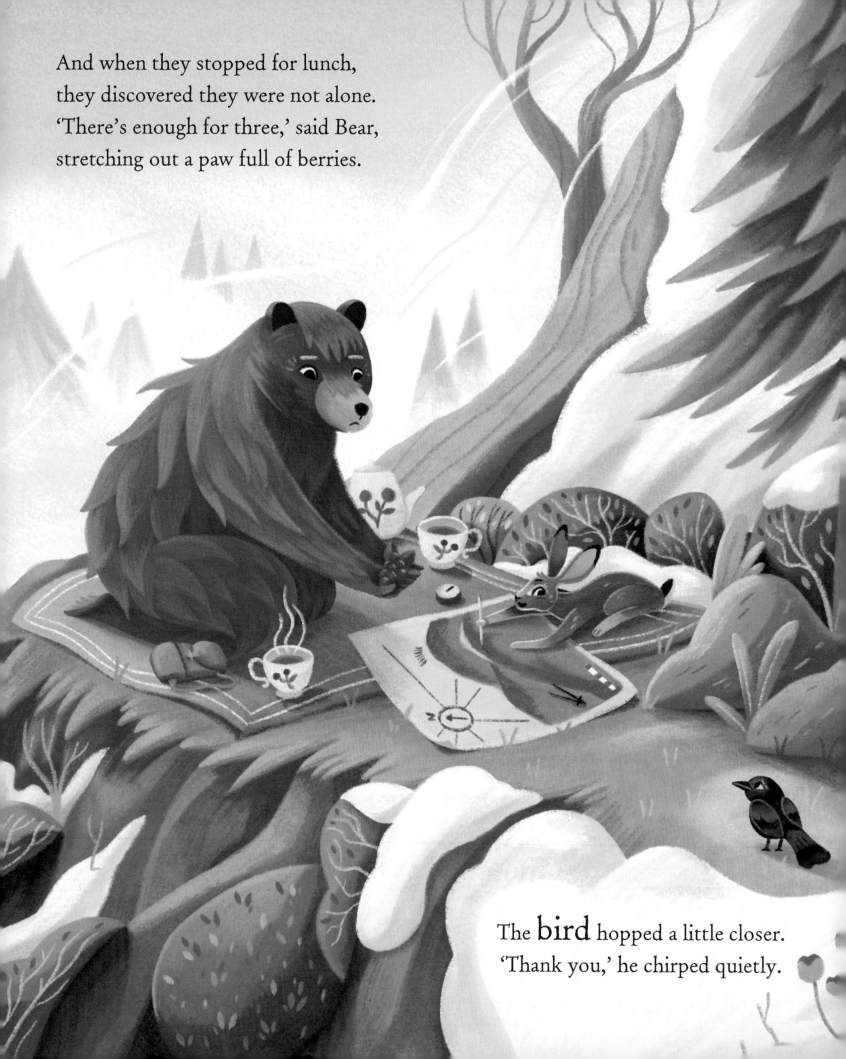

And when they stopped for lunch, they discovered they were not alone. 'There's enough for three,' said Bear, stretching out a paw full of berries.

The **bird** hopped a little closer. 'Thank you,' he chirped quietly.

'Are you looking for the **treasure** too?' asked Hare. 'Can't you just fly to the top?' asked Bear. Blackbird dipped his head. His feathers trembled.

'It's okay,' said Bear. 'Would you like to come with us instead?' And though Blackbird wanted to answer with a big, loud YES, he only managed a small, quiet nod.

On they climbed,
and the mountain was steep,
and creepy, and cold.

But the animals thought only
of the treasure.

Night brought wind
and rain and from somewhere,
a distant **howling**.

'AWOOOOOOO!'

Blackbird saw that the others
were afraid, so he took a long, deep breath...

and began to sing.
He filled the night with songs of springtime,
and watched their fear fade away.

And when the sun woke up, they carried on.
And though the mountain was steep,
and creepy, and cold, they
pushed forwards,

with Hare's spirit,

Bear's warmth,

and
Blackbird's
song.

And by the time they reached the top,
they'd almost forgotten about the treasure.
Until there, beneath eight tall, scraggly trees,
was an old wooden chest.

'There it is!'
pointed Bear.

'We've found it!'
said Blackbird.

'Are you ready?' asked Hare,
stepping closer to open the lid…

to nothing but a pair of wet
woodlice and a very relieved frog.

'That can't be it!' said Hare.
'There must be more...' said Bear.

They leaned in for a closer look...

and were amazed at what they saw.
'Are they really... us?'
asked Blackbird.

Night grew near, and the animals
shuffled down the mountain excitedly.
'Where shall we go next?'
asked Hare. 'The beach, the jungle?'

'I could sing to the fish,' chirped Blackbird, 'or the monkeys!'

'I don't mind where we go,' said Bear, 'as long as we go **together**.'

Lightning **crackled** above.
And from nearby, the **howling** came again.

But this time,
they thought it **beautiful**.
For they understood that the others were
also looking for the treasure that would
make their dreams come true. And like
them, had already found it.

Though they would
only realise it, once they opened
an old wooden chest, beneath
eight tall, scraggly trees, atop
a cold, dark mountain.

To Jon, for always believing. – M.F.

For Jewels, my treasure and guiding light. And
for my parents – I love you – and my siblings.
Also, Boxie – you are the cutest. – B.L.

MAGIC CAT PUBLISHING

The Treasure © 2024 Lucky Cat Publishing Ltd
Text © 2024 Marcela Ferreira
Illustrations © 2024 Brian Lambert
First Published in 2024 by Magic Cat Publishing, an imprint of Lucky Cat Publishing
Ltd, Unit 2 Empress Works, 24 Grove Passage, London E2 9FQ, UK

The right of Marcela Ferreira to be identified as the author of this work and Brian
Lambert to be identified as the illustrator of this work has been asserted by them in
accordance with the Copyright, Designs and Patents Act, 1988 (UK).

A catalogue record for this book is available from the British Library.

ISBN 978-1-913520-86-1

The illustrations were created digitally
Set in Old Claude LP

Published by Katie Cotton
Designed by Zoë Tucker

Manufactured in China

9 8 7 6 5 4 3 2 1

FSC
www.fsc.org

MIX
Paper from
responsible sources
FSC® C104723